D1365554

My Own Song

And Other Poems to Groove To

Selected by Michael R. Strickland

Illustrated by Eric Sabee

Wordsong
Boyds Mills Press

To Christa Lee Olson
For The Music

—M. S.

Published by Wordsong
Boyds Mills Press, Inc.
A Highlights Company
815 Church Street
Honesdale, Pennsylvania 18431
Printed in Mexico

Publisher Cataloging-in-Publication Data
My own song : and other poems to grove to / selected by Michael R.
Strickland ; illustrated by Eric Sabee.—1st ed.
[64]p. : ill. ; cm.
Summary : A collection of poems about music.
ISBN 1-56397-686-2
1. Music—Juvenile poetry. 2. Children's poetry. [1. Music—Poetry.
2. American Poetry—Collections.] I. Strickland, Michael. II. Sabee, Eric, ill. III. Title.
811.54—dc20 1997
Library of Congress Catalog Card Number 97-70582

First edition, 1997
Book designed by Tim Gillner
The text of this book is set in 12-point Palatino.
The illustrations are done in scratchboard.

10 9 8 7 6 5 4 3 2 1

Table of Contents

Section 1: A Party for the Ears

Section 2: A Rainbow of Musical Sights That Delight

Section 3: Songs That Touch the Body, Mind, and Heart

Section 4: Magical Movement and Lively Vibrations

A Party for the Ears

The Music Master

"My sons," said a Glurk slurping soup.
"We would make a fine musical group.
  Put your spoon to your lip
  And slurp when you sip.
But don't spill. Like this, children—*oop*!"

John Ciardi

Fiddler From Sasilli Street

I am Miquel the music maker.
I'm a minstrel of rhythm and beat.
I'm the neighborhood virtuoso.
I'm the fiddler from Sasilli Street.

I'm a lyrist. A flutist. A piper.
I'm a master of wood piccolos.
I'm a thigh-tapping tambourine player,
from the tip of my head to my toes.

I'm a do-re-mi harmonic hero.
I'm a street strolling band balladeer.
I'm a thumb strumming soft banjo picker,
who's a musical mad musketeer.

I am Miquel the music maker.
I was born with a horn in my hand.
I'm the prince of perfection with meter.
I'm a king in a musical land.

I'm a be-boppin, jazz-jammin' jingle,
with a traveling troubadours' beat.
I'm the maestro of musical magic.
I'm the fiddler from Sasilli Street.

Rebecca Kai Dotlich

Reggae Night

Hurry Hattie, reggae night
Hear the haunting drums loud beat.
Forget hard times, let's go dance;
We'll sway and stomp, kick up our feet.

Come on Hattie to our town hall.
The crowd of dancers starts to swell.
Shaking shoulders, winding hips,
Under reggae's magic spell.
Things gonna be all right.
Things gonna be all right.

Listen Hattie, hear the drums.
Watch the drummers' dreadlocks fly.
Entranced by their hypnotic beat
We'll rock to rhythmic reggae high.

Join in Hattie. To guitar strums
A singer wails Bob Marley's song.
Let's clap our hands, sing out too
Sing it loud, sing it strong;
Things gonna be all right.
Things gonna be all right.

Monica Gunning

Bell

By flat tink
Of tin, or thin
Copper tong,
Brass clang,
Bronze bong,

The bell gives
Metal a tongue—
To sing
In one sound
Its whole song.

Valerie Worth

Music

Can you dance?
I love to dance!
Music is my happy chance.
Music playing
In the street
Gets into
My hands and feet.

Can you sing?
I love to sing!
Music, like a bird in Spring,
With a gold
And silver note
Gets into
My heart and throat.

Can you play?
I'd love to play!
Practice music every day—
Then you'll give
The world a chance
To dance and sing
To sing and dance.

Eleanor Farjeon

An orangutan rang my doorbell

An orangutan rang my doorbell
So I asked him up to tea
The orangutan sat in my kitchen
Then the orangutan sang to me
I banged and twanged my banjo
The orangutan sang his song
We did the orangutan tango
And we diddle-danged all day long
If an orangutan rings your doorbell
Don't call the nearest zoo
Cause the orangutan's quite
A swinger and
He'll sing
His song
For you.

Sheree Fitch

Moon of Popping Trees

Outside the lodge,
the night air is bitter cold.
Now the Frost Giant walks
with his club in his hand.
When he strikes the trunks
of the cottonwood trees
we hear them crack
beneath the blow.
The people hide inside
when they hear that sound.

But Coyote, the wise one,
learned the giant's
magic song,
and when Coyote sang it,
the Frost Giant slept.

Now when the cottonwoods
crack with frost again
our children know, unless
they hear Coyote's song,
they must stay inside,
where the fire is bright
and buffalo robes
keep us warm.

Joseph Bruchac and Jonathan London

Boom Box Bart

Since he's so loud when he gets down,
  they made a noise law for the town.

They call him Boom Box Bart:
The kid is thunder.
He's lightning.
Rip roaring pouring rain.

A Panasonic
Megaphonic
CD hurricane.

They call him Boom Box Bart,
  10,000 watts a night,
DANGER DANGER
  for your eardrums,
  next best thing to dynamite.

Michael R. Strickland

The Touch-Tone Phone and the Xylophone

A touch-tone phone
Met a xylophone
As they strolled neath the moon
By the rolling sea.
Said the touch-tone phone
To the xylophone
"How I wish that a tune
Could be played on me."

"All I hear are voices,
Low ones, strong ones,
Gabble-gabble-gabble-gabble-
All day-long-ones,
While you, lucky friend,
Hear song after song
Of low notes, high notes,
Fast notes, slow notes."

"Oh, if only my buttons
Were bars or keys
That would sound like
Your plink-plank melodies."

Alice Low

Sing, sing, what shall we sing?

Sing, sing, what shall we sing?
A song to delight your ear.
Sing, sing, how shall we sing?
With a sound that is loud and clear.

Strum, strum, when shall we strum?
As we carry our fine guitars.
Strum, strum, where shall we strum?
By your window, under the stars.

Arnold Lobel

Change of Wind

Music is snobbish, too, alack! there are social classes
Even in Lydia, even on the green slopes of Parnassus
Some instruments are better tone than others, some are low
Strings are superior to brass and woodwind, did you know?
Strings are high-class, but wind players are an inferior set
Flute, oboe, trumpet, piccolo, horn, bassoon, and clarinet.

All this arose when night music was a commercial affair
You dined inside and the players serenaded in the open air
Except those instruments affected by damp such as strings
or tambour
Which were therefore privileged to come into the supper
chamber
But the wind players stood outside in the courtyard getting
wet:
Flute, oboe, trumpet, piccolo, horn, bassoon, and clarinet.

Mozart changed all that; some of his best friends played
the oboe
(Which in those days was a low occupation, little better
than being a hobo)
He wrote quartets for them, cassations, concerti, and
serenades,
Sinfonie concertante and divertimenti in positive
cascades

He lavished these musical offerings on them without stint
Despite the risk that no publisher would put such vulgar
stuff into print
Consideration like this had never been shown to them yet:
Flute, oboe, trumpet, piccolo, horn, bassoon, and clarinet.

Having a special fondness for clarinets, Mozart gladdened
their hearts
By going on to write piano concerti in which he gave them
marvelous parts
Almost equal to that of the soloist, an unheard-of thing
to do!
And then his friend Beethoven took hold of the notion and
did it too
So the wind players, hitherto such tag, rag, and bobtail
At last began to rise higher in the orchestral scale.
No longer would they have to stand outside in the dark
and wet
Flute, oboe, trumpet, piccolo, horn, bassoon, and clarinet.

Joan Aiken

I Got It Bad

for Ella Fitzgerald

Ella, you sing my soul
up and down your silky scale,
just enough smoke in your voice
to say something about sorrow:

in emotion like the ocean
it's either sink or swim,
when a woman loves a man
like I love him . . . .

No Billy Holliday, you
don't break a heart already broken,
but like a surgeon weave each note
in with the next, and out:

I got it bad and that ain't good,
my poor heart is sentimental
not made of wood—
I got it bad and that ain't good.

When you sing it, Ella,
your voice soothes and stitches
me back together strong.

Lisa Bahlinger

Dinosaur Hard Rock Band

Up on the stage is the dinosaur band
While waiting below, in the mud and the sand,
Are acres of dinosaurs who all demand,
"Sing 'Down in the Mudflats and Sharps'!"

The band members grin as they start on the tune,
With rock bass and rock drum and hard rock bassoon.
They sing up a storm out there under the moon,
Playing "Down in the Mudflats and Sharps."

Sandstone and shale are the rocks that they play.
You don't see a dinosaur rock band each day
With drums and a bass guitar wailing away
Playing "Down in the Mudflats and Sharps."

The band is long gone but the song still remains
Imprinted in bedrock that's found on the plains.
And when the wind whistles, it brings back the strains
Of "Down in the Mudflats and Sharps."

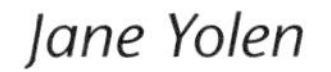

Jane Yolen

I Have To Stand By Susan Todd

I have to stand by Susan Todd?
That's the worst.
Not me.
I'd rather face
a firing squad.
Who said,
it must be
short to tall
at concerts,
alphabetical
would be more fair.
But please,
not me.
Not there.
Susan Todd can't
sing on key.

She sings so bad
my neck hairs jump.
Her voice creates
eardrum goosebumps.

It squints my eyes,
it curls my toes.
I know she tries
to find the notes,
but her screeching search
is like the scrape
of blackboards
by a metal rake.

Just this once?
Give me a break!

Sara Holbrook

A Rainbow of Musical Sights That Delight

Song of the Water Lilies

Sing a song of colors
of soft petals in sunlight
sing a muted lilies song
music blooms in the
still waters

Eloise Greenfield

First Bird Of Spring

You've seen so much
since you've been away,
sing me a song.

Sing of the mountains
you crossed last fall
through starry nights
and blazing dawns,

Of rivers, bayous,
checkerboard farms,
glistening silos,
pigeony barns.

Sing of lightning,
wind-tossed waves,
ships at anchor,
tranquil days.

You've seen so much
it will take all spring,
sing me a song.

David Harrison

Cuckoo Song

Summer is a-coming in,
Sing loud cuckoo!
The seed grows, the meadow blooms
And the woods spring up now—
Sing cuckoo!

Ewe bleats after lamb,
Cow lows after calf;
Bullock jumps, deer darts about,
Merrily sing cuckoo!

Cuckoo, cuckoo, you sing well, cuckoo:
Don't ever stop now;
Sing cuckoo, now, sing cuckoo,
Sing cuckoo, sing cuckoo, now!

Author unknown
translated by Kenneth Koch

Wellington the Skeleton

A skeleton called Wellington
Lives in my dresser drawer
Though every time I open it
He's just a pinafore.

But when I close it, he becomes
A lonesome soloist,
And Wellington the Skeleton
Gets up and does the Twist!

I hear him shake and rattle, like
A living castanet.
I've memorized the sound, although
I haven't seen him yet—

Cause every time I open it
The light gets in once more,
And Wellington the Skeleton
Is just a pinafore.

O Wellington the Skeleton,
We both know you exist:
Why won't you come outside and do
The living, breathing Twist?

I know that I'm alive, and you
Are dead as dead can be:
But a skeleton gets lonely in a
Dresser, just like me.

And as for me, I figure I'll
Be bony too one day.
Why don't we get together, while
We still have time to play?

Dennis Lee

Maybe Next Year

We marched onto the field for the band competition.
The polished brass instruments shined bright,
 our uniforms pressed, medium starched,
 steady formation,
 esprit de corps tight.

We stood ready to go on yard line one,
 and marched in place on the taut green turf.
When the drums rolled:
 RAT-TAT-TAT-TAT
 we felt charged,
 while the sun
 heated the fur of the drum major's hat.

Then trumpeters, tubas, and flautists began.
The large crowd clapped and clapped again.
Flags unfurled,
 batons twirled through the air.
After practicing weeks and weeks,
 right there on that field,
 it was finally our turn to compete.

When suddenly:

 it rained,
 and rained,
 and rained.

All I can guess,
 if I do have to say,
is that someone somewhere,
 up there in the clouds,
just did not want us to play that day.

Michael R. Strickland

Sonnet 130

My mistress' eyes are nothing like the sun;
Coral is far more red than her lips' red:
If snow be white, why then her breasts are dun;
If hairs be wires, black wires grow on her head. 4
I have seen roses damask'd, red and white,
But no such roses see I in her cheeks;
And in some perfumes is there more delight
Than in the breath that from my mistress reeks. 8
I love to hear her speak, yet well I know
That music hath a far more pleasing sound:
I grant I never saw a goddess go;
My mistress, when she walks, treads on the ground: 12
And yet, by heaven, I think my love as rare
As any she belied with false compare.

William Shakespeare

Changes

Albums, tapes and thin CD's.
Music plays on all of these.
Through the years
the styles have changed,
the look, the size,
it's rearranged,
but one thing always
stays the same—
the love
of the beat
is the name
of the game.

Rebecca Kai Dotlich

The Singer of the Night

Sunset fade while shadows creep
Lay down your head and sleep sweet sleep
The singer of night sings wise and deep

To all things of the dark he calls
To slip outside their hidden walls

All through the hours slow and deep
He weaves his music through your sleep
While insects hum and small things creep

Lay down your head and sleep sweet sleep
The singer of night sings wise and deep
Lay down your head and sleep.

David Harrison

After Mass in Georgia

Red dogwood trees turn the air the way fans
in church keep the hymns moving.

A boy stares longingly at an empty softball field,
arms hooked into the wire fence, he pulls

off his cap as a girl wipes her forehead,
her body, reflecting up from the bottom

of a glass of water, trembles with color
and light. Flattened spoons clatter

and turn, squaredancers. Wind is the caller,
makes its own music. This is not a photograph.

Only a waterglass balanced on a porch rail,
a glass brimming with light. Overhead, chimes.

Lisa Bahlinger

Conversation

Are you happy?

I can't say. But let me tell you
about my sunflowers,
the seeds I held in yesterday's hand . . .

You could crush them in your teeth,
so brittle, seeming solid . . .

I buried them and today they burst open
like music, or something I needed to say—
the golden orange notes curl as if tacked
to brown pincushions.

so, the heads nod over you
as if on thick, green ropes?

I looked up and saw them,
they who are perfect—

Ah, they take nothing from you.

They give nothing but themselves.

Lisa Bahlinger

We four lads from Liverpool are

We four lads from Liverpool are:
Paul in a taxi, John in a car,
George on a scooter, tootin' his hooter,
Following Ringo Starr!

Author unknown

Songs That Touch the Body, Mind, and Heart

Song of Wonder

When the room is dark,
  and the world's asleep,
  I lean into the night
  with
  wonder:

  what makes things wonderful?
  So many great stories,
  so much music, rhyme, rhythm,
  why the love of my family
  and glorious playtime?

I wonder:
  Am I a miracle?
  And why does my mother sing "My darling child"
  when she tucks me in tight,
  with an angel's glow by the tiny nightlight?

Why is life magical?
  I can pretend to ride my bike through outer space,
  or dream up friends who play for days,
  are always happy,
  and do everything I like.

I wake to wonder,
  and the morning bird in the nearest tree
  whistles happiness,
  watches me.

Michael R. Strickland

A Mother's Hope

I lie next to your sweet body
transfixed by your innocent sleep.
Your lips sing the silent rhythms
of infancy while I whisper
an old lullaby.

I am afraid, I am afraid
I may not be up to the task
of being a mother.
I am afraid my scars will
tarnish your life
and my sorrow will steal
the sunlight when you awaken
tomorrow.

But tomorrow, tomorrow won't have
the sour taste of yesterday's tears.
Tomorrow I will be happy,
tomorrow I will save myself.
Tomorrow I will cry
and my sobs will make
music
and my words
will make
poetry.

Tomorrow I will
hold you in my arms
and the past will be a painting
on the wall.

Tomorrow your plant will
blossom and
grow strong—
a song
for the garden
I gave you.

Edvige Giunta

Rose-cheeked Laura

Rose-cheeked Laura, come,
Sing thou smoothly with thy beauty's
Silent music, either other
        Sweetly gracing.

Lovely forms do flow
From concent divinely framed;
Heav'n is music, and thy beauty's
        Birth is heavenly.

These dull notes we sing
Discords need for helps to grace them;
Only beauty purely loving
        Knows no discord,

But still moves delight,
Like clear springs renewed by flowing,
Ever perfect, ever in them-
        Selves eternal.

Thomas Campion

Song

How sweet I roam'd from field to field,
    And tasted all the summer's pride,
'Till I the prince of love beheld,
    Who in the sunny beams did glide!

He shew'd me lilies for my hair,
    And blushing roses for my brow;
He led me through his gardens fair,
    Where all his golden pleasures grow.

With sweet May dews my wings were wet,
    And Phoebus fir'd my vocal rage;
He caught me in his silken net,
    And shut me in his golden cage.

He loves to sit and hear me sing,
    Then, laughing, sports and plays with me;
Then stretches out my golden wing,
    And mocks my loss of liberty.

William Blake

The Singing Beggars

singing beggars
in the street
dancing
and asking for
money
singing beggars
in the street
dancing
and asking for
money. one

is dancing
on his hands another
juggles pins a third

with the face of an ape
tells a dirty joke. then
the policeman arrives

and they all make fun of him. this
is the science of poverty
in action, the perfect
balance of three worlds. how can that

poor cop possibly know that,
trying to grasp their collars
and coming up
with air?

Cornelius Eady

Celebrate

Raise
your hands.
Wiggle
your fingers.
Jump right up,
and let go!
Raise
your voice and
clap
to a beat.
Beam
a smile.
Shout
and
dance.
Ring
chimes and bells.
Prance
about and
sing.
Spread
your joy
to the world.

It's time to
raise
your hands.

Michael R. Strickland

Nocturnal Dance

for Josh

I cling
to the shapeless hands
of dark trees
to begin my nocturnal walk.

I carve a pink moon
into perfectly round slices
and lay them down to cover
the thin air of late spring.

I wrap my feet in old leaves
to journey into the night.
Will you come
with me?

My heart beats
to the rhythm of an old song.
I invite you to join
me in an old dance
and we move slowly, out of tune
like clumsy bears.

You linger on the threshold
of this strange land,
I offer you wilted daisies
to wipe the fear from your eyes
and guide you inside
a red-roofed house.

I feed you strawberries and oranges
dripping their red sweetness
on your lips.

You smell the past
in my hair.

Edvige Giunta

Piano Lessons

i used to sit at piano lessons
and cry
or hear my sisters crying
in the other room.
the old woman would snap
and say tight-lipped
"you are no good. what is wrong
with you."
but every year she would invite us
to her dogs' birthday party.
only the dogs got hats.
and in the summer
her funny smell would fill
the screen porch
where we waited our turns
to be defeated.
i would sit in the hammock
with the green terry cover.
and the candy in those
crystal dishes
(we never really knew if it
was there to eat)
it always tasted a million years old.

Candy Clayton

Way Down in the Music

I get way down in the music
Down inside the music
I let it wake me
                    take me
Spin me around and make me
Uh-get down

Inside the sound of the Jackson Five
Into the tune of Earth, Wind and Fire
Down in the bass where the beat comes from
Down in the horn and down in the drum
I get down
I get down

I get down in the music
Down inside the music
I let it wake me
                    take me
Spin me around and shake me
I get down, down
I get down

Eloise Greenfield

Sing

Sail
your
ship in
gentle
wind

easy-
going
person

live
free
to love

laughter
often
inside
of your
song

sing

seek
and
know
peace.

Michael R. Strickland

Night Sister

Mascarpone and coffee mingle
amorously
and my lips full of anticipation
savor the sudden sweetness
of blood
on a winter night
when the past broke the windowpanes
of my soul.

Golden strings pierce my skin
but their music leaves me deaf
and numb.

The heavy thump of feet
and the force of words
that scratch the heart
like broken fingernails
is all you can offer,
nightly creature.

There's no healing, no going back,
no remembering, no forgetting,
no candles on my cake.

All that is left is the humming
of wounded sparrows.

Edvige Giunta

Fiddle Practice

I guess you know
Some girls are slow
When it's time for fiddle practice.
Their arms get stiff.
They act as if
They had swallowed a dry cactus.
They don't feel well.
Yes, they can tell
They're about to catch a cold.
Well, that's when I
and Mummy try
To say (and *not to scold*):

Your arms are *not* stiff.
Your throat is *not* sore.
But something, we think, is going to be *if*
We have to tell you this *once more*:
IT'S TIME! So get your fiddle and bow.
And get your excuses done.
And practice that piece you're supposed to know
And haven't even begun!

In an hour or so
She puts her bow
To the strings and saws away.
And it sounds all right
For, say, a catfight.
But I couldn't exactly say
That note for note
It's what anyone wrote.
That's when I catch Mummy's eye.

And we shudder a bit
At the sound of it.
And both of us wonder why
We make her do
What she's doing to

The music someone wrote.
And we stuff our ears.
And we say, "Three cheers!"
When we come to the last—well—note:
Let's call it that.
For sharp or flat,
Or squeak, or squawk, or squeeeee,
It's done for today.
And I'm here to say
That's good enough for me.

John Ciardi

O Black and Unknown Bards

O black and unknown bards of long ago,
  How came your lips to touch the sacred fire?
How, in your darkness, did you come to know
  The power and beauty of the minstrel's lyre?
Who first from midst his bonds lifted his eyes?
  Who first from out the still watch, lone and long,
Feeling the ancient faith of prophets rise
  Within his dark-kept soul, burst into song?

There is a wide, wide wonder in it all,
  That from degraded rest and servile toil
The fiery spirit of the seer should call
  These simple children of the sun and soil.
O black slave singers, gone, forgot, unfamed,
  You—you, alone, of all the long, long line
Of those who've sung untaught, unknown, unnamed,
Have stretched out upward, seeking the divine.

James Weldon Johnson

In the kitchen, Kalilah's jazzercise

While she danced, I swear
a jazzy breeze
ran through her flowing hair.
Her arms told a story, moving
to the harmonious rhythm of her body.
I'm telling you:
if her silk blouse (red)
was a caress, her skirt stiffly
announced determination! freedom!
She might have moved
with conviction and strength,
or was it
softly, the dance
a billowing current of cool,
cool air?

Arnetta Johnson

The Silver Swan Who Living had No Note

The silver swan, who living had no note,
When death approached unlocked her silent throat;
Leaning her breast against the reedy shore,
Thus sung her first and last, and sung no more.
Farewell, all joys; O death, come close mine eyes;
More geese than swans now live, more fools than wise.

Anonymous

MAGICAL MOVEMENT AND LIVELY VIBRATIONS

Hummingbird

A hummingbird flies standing still
and never sings a note.

His whirling wings make circles,
little helicopter circles
making music of their own:

  a whirry sound
  a blurry sound
  a feathers in a flurry sound.

How can anything that is so small
make such a great big hurry sound?

Jacqueline Sweeney

Those Who Do Not Dance

An invalid girl asked,
"How do I dance?"
We told her:
let your heart dance.

Then the crippled girl asked,
"How do I sing?"
We told her:
let your heart sing.

A poor dead thistle asked,
"How do I dance?"
We told it,
let your heart fly in the wind.

God asked from on high,
"How do I come down from this blueness?"
We told Him:
come dance with us in the light.

The entire valley is dancing
in a chorus under the sun.
The hearts of those absent
return to ashes.

Gabriela Mistral

Dinosaur Waltz

The lights are all lit
At the Dino café,
While overhead chandeliers
Shiver and sway.
And everyone knows
To get out of the way
When dinosaurs,
dinosaurs waltz.

The chairs are pushed back
And the tables are, too.
The pies put away
By the smart café crew.
The clock on the wall
Strikes a quarter to two
When dinosaurs,
dinosaurs waltz.

The music begins
With its one-two-three beat,
And then comes the sound
Of those dinosaur feet,
A rhythm that pounds
All the way down the street
When dinosaurs,
dinosaurs waltz.

One-two-three, one-two-three,
And there they go,
Whirling and twirling
And swirling just so,
Each dinosaur lass
With her dinosaur beau
When dinosaurs,
dinosaurs waltz.

I'll never forget
The first time I was there:
You wore a red rose
In your dinosaur hair,
And I would have kissed you,
But I didn't dare
When dinosaurs,
dinosaurs waltz.

The music goes slow
And the music goes fast,
Just like dino love which,
Alas, does not last,
But leaves its imprint
On the stones of the past
When dinosaurs,
dinosaurs waltz.

Jane Yolen

Moon Dance

Beneath a pale
moon we're dancing,
sweeping over
starlit lawns.
In the stillness
voices echo—
put your dancing slippers on
So heel to toe
we spin and slide,
galloping in
a circle-ride
To the hum of a cello,
the chime of a bell,
we're a caprioling
carousel, a merry-midnight
romping rhyme,
stepping in
and out of time,
sweeping over
starlit lawns—
put your dancing slippers on.

Rebecca Kai Dotlich

Market-Square Dance

Once a year all the villagers dance.
Excitement is in the air.
Music is in the air.
Food aromas fill the air.

The fanfare is a big sight for our eyes.
The spirit of the village
Blazes brightly like a star.
Like monsters the villagers dress,
But, sweetly, like saints, they sing.

Play up the music!
Dance, dance, village folks, jump up high!
In circles, around and around,
Weaving with one another
Like a twirling whirlpool.

Children in grass skirts
Rollick with wild enthusiasm
To the din of handbells,
The clattering of dried gourds
Wrapped with strings of cowries,
And to the clapping of hands.
Their eyes beam
And their hearts beat
To the boom
Of double-barreled drums.

Play up the music!
Dance, dance, village folks,
  jump up high!
With joy they bow,
Leap
Twirl
Twist
Bend forward
Bend backward
Shake, shake, shake!

Isaac Olaleye

Into Mother's slide trombone

Into Mother's slide trombone
Liz let fall her ice-cream cone.
Now when marching, Mother drips
Melting notes and chocolate chips.

X. J. Kennedy

My Own Song

My radio pumps out a tune,
   awakes me to compose my day.
7:15
I must rush
Toast and an apple are the first two notes,
before a mad tango to the bus.

In history class I become Lincoln,
   with a paper beard and top hat.
Or in my suit
   preach Malcolm X,
   or with the feathers of Chief Seattle in my hair:
   yell and dance,
"Save our Land!"
What a show I am,
   singing operas about the past,
I make my own future song.

I read magazines, books, stories, poems
   and keep writing my own song,
   more melodious every day.

The bell rings in lunch,
   and hip-hop talk with pals at the table,
   then kill-the-kid-with-the-ball,
   on the lawn,
   Until it rings again.
Then it's back to rock-and-roll,
   with the punches of math and science.

Handel's *Hallelujah* Chorus sounds:
My school day is complete.

I'm free to conduct the afternoon,
a symphony of fun.

My bicycle orchestra shall play my favorite overture,
the one about racing after school,
to the peaks of asphalt mountains.

Until the darkness that's not half as scary as
Mom's baritone yell at us to get back by dinner.

Then I pound out my rhythm of family time:
computer games,
snacks, homework,
fighting for the bathrooms
and the T.V. remote control.
Occasionally missing a chord
with my big brother
but I try to harmonize and keep the beat,
until I take a bow
and go to sleep.

Michael R. Strickland

The Distant Talking Drum

From deep in the rain forest
The sound of a distant talking drum I hear—
Far away, far away.
For me it calls.
Clearly it calls
For me to dance,
For men to dance,
For women to dance,
For children to dance.

And the sound of the distant drum
Echoes through the rain forest.
The distant talking drum
Is calling across the mighty rain forest
For me to come,
For me to dance.
Now the sound of sweet songs
I hear.
Beautifully they flow!

And the distant talking drum
Is still calling
Far away, far away.
Clearly it calls
For me to come,
For me to dance.
So across the rain forest,
The wide, wild, and wonderful rain forest,
I go!

Isaac Olaleye

Slim Slater

Slim Slater lives in a camper
That serves as a house and car,
And, in his movable household
That carries him near and far,
He keeps no extra possessions
Except for a green guitar.

Before Slim travels each morning
Through sunshine or rain or snow,
He strokes his guitar a minute,
Then strums it an hour or so,
And sings to his strumming music
A ballad called "Here we go."

And when he stops in the evening
He squints at the first white star
And—even before his supper—
He picks up his green guitar
And sings to the dusk or sunset
A ballad called "Here we are."

And, since he has no com-
  panions
To keep him from being free,
When people who hear his
  ballads
Ask: "Who does he mean by
  'We'?"
Slim Slater quietly answers,
"My camper, guitar, and me."

So Slim, with countries to
  cover,
Continues to ride and roam,
And whether he drives his
  camper
To Mexico, Maine, or Nome,
Slim Slater is never homesick
Because he is always home.

Kaye Starbird

John Canoe Dancers

Raggedy costumes in a collage of colors,
metals and tin cans hanging,
John Canoe dancers
at Christmastime
whirl down the road.

Masks like devils or horses' heads,
waving pitchforks and sticks,
John Canoe dancers
jig down the road
to their fife and drums.

Watching them from a distance,
their clanging comes closer.
One lunges at me!
I run screaming from
the John Canoe dancers.

Monica Gunning

A Dancer

A dancer
is what I will be,
I watch them on T. V.
I spin and dip with arms stretched wide,
and leave the ground,
so high a leap
my flying feet are out of reach.
I make no sounds
when I touch down.
I float, I flutter,
I bow to the ground.

The music is what takes me up,
in slow, in sweeping strokes,
until it's fast and red and wild,
then I jump-snap-kick.
I'm faster than a drummer
beating with six sticks.

I practice everyday in my own living room.
Surely someday soon,
the dancers on T. V.,
they really will be me.

Sara Holbrook

The compiler of *My Own Song and Other Poems to Groove To* wishes to thank the following authors, publishers, and agents for permission to reprint copyrighted material. Every possible effort has been made to trace the ownership of each poem included. If any errors or omissions have occurred, corrections will be made in subsequent printings, provided the publisher is notified of their existence.

"Change of Wind" from *Skin Spinners* by Joan Aiken. Copyright © 1976 by Joan Aiken. Reprinted with permission from Brandt & Brandt Literary Agents, Inc. "After Mass in Georgia" and "Conversation" by Lisa Bahlinger. Copyright © 1996 by Lisa Bahlinger. Reprinted by permission of the author. "I Got it Bad" by Lisa Bahlinger. Copyright © 1996 by Lisa Bahlinger. Reprinted with permission from the author. Excerpts from "I Got It Bad (and That Ain't Good)" by Duke Ellington and Paul Francis Webster reprinted with permission from EMI Records and Webster Music Co. "Moon of Popping Trees" from *Thirteen Moons on Turtle's Back* by Joseph Bruchac and Jonathan London. Copyright © 1982 by Joseph Bruchac and Jonathan London. Reprinted by permission of Philomel Books. "Fiddle Practice" from *The Monster Den* by John Ciardi. Copyright © 1963, 1964, 1966 by John Ciardi. Copyright renewed 1991 by Judith H. Ciardi. Reprinted wtih permission from Boyds Mills Press. "The Music Master" from *Someone Could Win a Polar Bear* by John Ciardi. Copyright © 1964, 1965, 1967, 1970 by John Ciardi. Reprinted with permission from Boyds Mills Press. "Piano Lessons" by Candy Clayton appeared in *Minnesota Poetry Outloud*, 2nd Season—1975, John Calvin Rezmerski, Editor. Extensive research failed to locate the author and/or copyright holder of this work. "Changes," "Fiddler from Sassili Street," and "Moon Dance" by Rebecca Kai Dotlich. Copyright © 1996. Reprinted with permission from the author. "The Singing Beggars" from *Kartunes* by Cornelius Eady. Copyright © 1980 by Cornelius Eady. Reprinted with permission from the author. "Music" from *Poems for Children* by Eleanor Farjeon. Copyright © 1938 by Eleanor Farjeon, renewed 1966 by Gervase Farjeon. Reprinted with permission from Harold Ober Associates, Inc. "An Orangutan Rang My Doorbell" from *Toes in My Nose* by Sheree Fitch. Copyright © 1987 by Sheree Fitch. Reprinted with permission from Boyds Mills Press. "A Song of Hope," "Night Sister," and "Nocturnal Dance" by Edvidge Giunta. Copyright © 1996 by Edvidge Giunta. Reprinted with permission from the author. "Song of the Water Lilies" from *Under the Sunday Tree* by Eloise Greenfield. Copyright © 1978 by Eloise Greenfield. Reprinted with permission of HarperCollins Publishers. "Way Down in the Music" from *Honey I Love* by Eloise Greenfield. Copyright © 1978 by Eloise Greenfield. Reprinted with permission from HarperCollins Publishers. "John Canoe Dancers" from *Not a Copper Penny in Me House* by Monica Gunning. Copyright © 1993 by Monica Gunning. Reprinted with permission from Boyds Mills Press. "Raggae Night" by Monica Gunning. Copyright © 1996 by Monica Gunning. Reprinted with permission from the author. "First Bird of Spring" by David Harrison. Copyright © 1996 by David Harrison. Reprinted by permission of Boyds Mills Press. "The Singer of Night" from *If Stars Had Strings* by David Harrison. Copyright © 1996 by David Harrison. Reprinted with permission from Boyds Mills Press. "A Dancer" from *Which Way to the Dragon!* by Sara Holbrook. Copyright © 1996 by Sara Holbrook. Reprinted with permission from Boyds Mills Press. "I Have to Stand by Susan Todd" from *Nothing's the End of the World* by Sara Holbrook. Copyright © 1995 by Sara Holbrook. Reprinted with permission from Boyds Mills Press. "In the Kitchen, Kalilah's Jazzercise" by Arnetta Johnson. Copyright © 1996 by Arnetta Johnson. Reprinted with permission from the author. "Sneaking in on soundless sneakers" from *Drat These Brats* by X. J. Kennedy. Copyright © 1993 by X. J. Kennedy. Reprinted by permission of Margaret K. McElderry Books, an imprint of Simon & Schuster Children's Publishing Division. Also preprinted by permission of Curtis Brown Ltd. "Cuckoo Song" from *Rose, Where Did You Get That Red?* by Kenneth Koch. Copyright © 1973, 1990 by Kenneth Koch. Reprinted with permission from Random House, Inc. "Wellington the Skeleton" from *Nicholas Knock and Other People* by Dennis Lee. Copyright © 1974 by Dennis Lee. Reprinted with permission from Macmillan of Canada Ltd. "Sing, sing, what shall we sing?" from *Whiskers and Rhymes* by Arnold Lobel. Copyright © 1985 by Arnold Lobel. Reprinted by permission from Greenwillow Books, a division of William Morrow, Inc. "The Touch Tone Phone and the Xylophone" by Alice Low. Copyright © 1995 by Alice Low. Reprinted with permission from the author. "Those Who Do Not Dance" by Gabriela Mistral in *Gabriela Mistral: A Reader*, edited by Marjorie Agosin, translated by Maria Giachetti. Copyright © 1993. Translation copyright © 1993 by Maria Giachetti. Reprinted with permission from White Pine Press. "The Distant Talking Drum" and "Market Square Dance" from *The Distant Talking Drum* by Isaac Olaleye. Copyright © 1995 by Isaac Olaleye. Reprinted with permission from Boyds Mills Press. "Hummingbird" from *Teaching Poetry: Yes You Can* by Jacqueline Sweeney. Copyright © 1993 by Jacqueline Sweeney. Reprinted by permission of Marian Reiner for the author. "Slim Slater" from *The Covered Bridgehouse* by Kaye Starbird. Reprinted by permission of Scholastic Inc. "bell" from *Still More Small Poems* by Valerie Worth. Copyright © 1978 by Valerie Worth. Reprinted by permission by of Farrar, Strauss & Giroux. "Dinosaur Hard Rock Band" and "Dinosaur Waltz" from *Dinosaur Dances* by Jane Yolen. Copyright © 1990 by Jane Yolen. Reprinted by permission of Curtis Brown Ltd.